A collage of original artwork
by Elizabeth Owens,
the creator of Nana Star

to

from

There's a mistake in *Nana Star*!
Can you find it for her?
You can if you pay attention to the words as you read along.

Send Nana Star a note correcting the mistake and become an honorary member of the ***Nana Star Little Twinkles Club***! You will receive an 8 x 10 photo of the real Nana Star with her special message just for you.

Send your note to:
ee publishing & productions, inc.
the laugh-friendly company ™
P.O. Box 8585
Albany, NY 12208

And remember to include your address!

All *Nana Star* stories feature a mistake because Nana Star believes that in life we all make mistakes, yet even with those mistakes, we can still create something beautiful. She reminds us that only God can make all things perfect!

Nana Star

written by Elizabeth Sills and Elena Patrice

illustrated by Linda Saker

ee publishing & productions, inc.

the laugh-friendly company[TM]

springfield, va 22151

Book design by Linda Saker

The book is typeset in Century Schoolbook

Illustrations are rendered in watercolor and ink on illustration board

Printed in the United States of America

Library of Congress Catalog Card Number: 2004093610

Nana Star

U.S. Edition 2004

ISBN 0-9753843-0-9

Summary: A little girl finds a fallen baby star. Together they begin a journey to return the star to its home.

In loving memory of

Cindy and Vance

Once upon a time in a land of swaying green grass and wildflowers, there was a little girl.

Now this little girl, like all little girls, was oh so very pretty. She wore a princess dress blue as the ocean waves.

A matching bow held back the curl in her hair. She
had a twinkle in her eye as she skipped with a bounce
in her step.

Her favorite place was among these fields of wildflowers where the air was sweet and the wind was warm.

"Hello, yellow sun!"

"Hello, puffy white clouds!"

"Will you play with me today?" the little girl asked.

"Are you a bird?"

"Is that a tree?" she guessed as she stared up at the shapes of the clowds.

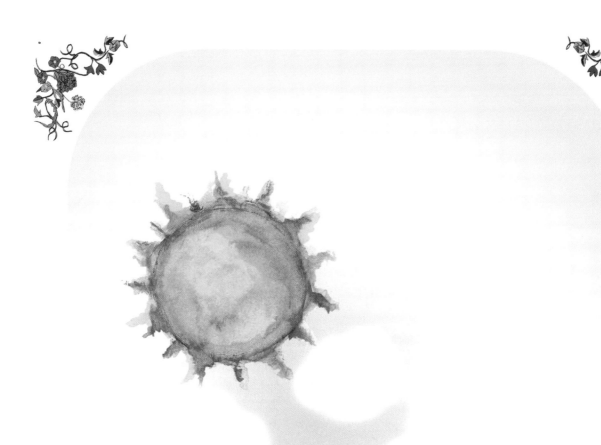

As her afternoon of imaginary fun came to an end,
the little girl drifted off into a peaceful nap.

The little girl was awakened by the tickle of a butterfly on her nose. Suddenly, off in the distance, she heard a faint call.

The little girl was very curious. She followed the sound all the way to a big green orchard of olive trees.

"Nana?" a quiet voice called out. "Nana?"

"Where are you?" asked the little girl.

"Here I am," said the meek voice.

As the little girl spun around, she saw a faint glow among a pile of leaves.

With great excitement, she ran to the pile and delicately removed each leaf.

There, before her eyes, lay a tiny baby star.

The little girl gently lifted the quivering, tiny star.

"Nana?" asked the star.

"Oh, you must be lost," said the little girl. "Don't be scared."

"Star, you belong up in the heavens." And she pointed to the sky.

"Nana . . .?" asked the tiny star with tears in his eyes.

"Don't cry, tiny star. I'll be your Nana until we find a way to get you back home."

As the tiny star rested in her pocket, the little girl wondered how she could help him feel closer to home.

She heard a whisper through the trees.

"Take one of my branches to lift your new friend towards the place he knows," said a wise old tree.

The little girl reached up, took a sturdy branch, and thanked the tree for his kindness.

"Please star, take hold of the end of this branch. I will carry you with me as we take this journey together."

The tiny baby star wrapped himself around the branch. The little girl held the branch high. The star was happy.

And so it begins, the story of Nana Star.

Elizabeth Owens
Nana Star

Elizabeth Owens is the creator of Nana Star and to those who know and love her, she is the real Nana Star. Born February 1, 1924 in Baltimore, Maryland, Elizabeth has three children, five grandchildren, and five great-grandchildren. Along with her cat, Jason, she lives in Germantown, Maryland, where she faithfully cares for many furry and feathered friends.

Elizabeth had a very special relationship with her grandson, Vance. Together they stood by the bedroom window at night, gazing at the stars. Vance often asked his Nana, "Is the Moonman really out there?" Nana told him that the Moonman was always there for him. When Vance moved away, Elizabeth sent him hand-crafted cards made of construction paper and illustrated with numerous darling characters drawn with markers and decorated with colorful stickers. She became "Nana Star" and, with the Moonman and many other friends, watched over Vance. This was Elizabeth's way of showing Vance that she was always with him.

Over time, an enchanting collection of thoughtful cards and other remembrances inspired by Nana Star came into being. The sweet and captivating characters in this collection touched the hearts of everyone who saw them.

Now four generations are involved in sharing the magic of Nana Star for others to enjoy. Elizabeth is the creator; her eldest daughter, Linda, is the illustrator; her granddaughters, elizabeth and elena, are the writers and publishers of this book; and her great-grandchildren, Allie, Nicky, and Julienne, have been insightful contributors to this special undertaking.

Elizabeth created Nana Star out of a great love for Vance and a desire to give him a sense of home wherever he was. Today, she hopes to extend that same love and feeling of belonging to children everywhere, in dedication to Vance, who now dances among the stars.